# A Small Medium at Large

R. A. Gates

Published by Stonehenge Circle Press, 2025.

A SMALL MEDIUM AT LARGE

**First edition. April 18, 2025.**

Copyright © 2025 R. A. Gates.

ISBN: 978-1680127522

Written by R. A. Gates.

This story is dedicated to my daughter, Angela, one of the most magical people I know.

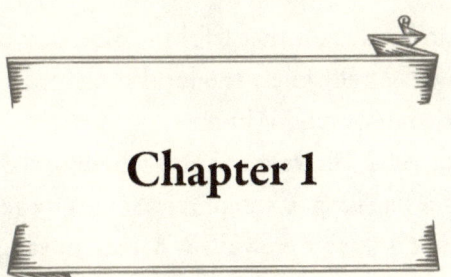

# Chapter 1

The bell above the front door of The Dragon's Lair Bookstore dinged. Laney glanced over from ringing up a customer to see Kody step inside. She smiled at her friend as he limped over to the front counter, his cane tapping along the hard wood. He stopped to scoop up a book lying open on the floor. He set it on top of one of the many piles of books squatting along the walls, waiting for their spot on a shelf to open up. He pulled out the stool that Mrs. Burns, the bookstore owner, had bought just for him. The metal legs scraped over the floor.

"One second," Laney whispered to him as she ripped the receipt from the old cash register. She put it in the bag along with the used copy of *101 Uses for Shrunken Heads*. She handed it to her customer. "Here you go, Mrs. Zon. I hope your husband feels better soon."

The old woman merely grunted as she took the bag.

As soon as she left the store, Laney shifted her attention to Kody. His black hair hung over his eyes like it usually did, and she had to fight the urge to brush it back. "Hey."

He glanced up from his phone and flashed her his crooked smile. "Hey." His phone buzzed in his hand. He frowned as he checked his text.

"What's wrong?" she asked.

"Nothing." He typed a quick message and then shoved his phone back in his pocket. "It's just Mr. McGregor wanting to know where I am. He's so annoying."

"Why does he care?" Kody had only joined the local werewolf pack a few months back when he and his family moved to Salmagundi after an encounter with an Eradicator that left him lame. Maybe Mr. McGregor didn't trust him yet. Laney knew the local pack leader was intense, but this seemed a little nosy, even for him.

"Because the sheriff will want to know where all the werewolves were if someone else goes missing. It's so unfair. Some guy gets eaten and they automatically think it was a werewolf. What about vampires, or ogres, or bears?"

"Oh, my," Laney said. "Did someone actually get eaten?"

Kody shrugged. "They found a big toe floating in the Salmagundi Bay."

"Really? That sounds like it could've been a mermaid. Have you seen the teeth on those guys?" She shuddered at the memory of her encounter with one when she'd been harvesting sea herbs for potions class last year. It had nearly chewed through the bars of the shark cage she was in. Thankfully, her teacher had been quick with a stunning spell.

"Apparently, the local pack of mermaids are migrating south right now."

"Gossip."

"No, it's true."

Laney's cheeks warmed as she explained. "A group of mermaids is called a gossip." *Why do I always have to correct people? He probably thinks I'm some pedantic nerd.*

"Oh, cool." Kody slouched while leaning on his cane. "I still can't believe mermaids are real, and that they would rather have me as a snack than a boyfriend."

Laney reached over the counter and patted him on the shoulder. Hollywood sanitized many magical creatures giving Banes, non-magical people, the wrong impressions. Kody had only been infected with lycanthropy a few years ago and therefore didn't grow up knowing anything about magic. Just wait until he learned the truth about unicorns.

"Did you hear about the latest missing person?" Kody asked. "That half troll/man guy, Steven...? Stanley...?"

"You mean Randy?"

"Yeah! He hasn't been seen for days now."

"Do you think it was Randy's big toe floating in the bay?"

Kody shrugged.

"I wonder what happened to the rest of him."

"Who knows? Of course, the sheriff searched the boarding house to see if he 'visited' recently." He added air quotes to emphasize his disgust.

Laney clenched her jaw to keep herself from going on a rant about the injustice of it all. It wasn't something Kody hadn't thought of or complained about before, so she decided to change the subject and get his mind off all that. "Want to see my new book? I found it in the last shipment."

"Sure." Kody sat up straighter on his stool.

Laney reached under the counter and pulled out her latest treasure. She set the used book in front of him so he could read the cover, *Speaking to Specters* by G Reaper. "Cool, huh. It has chapters about how to conduct a seance and the proper etiquette when speaking with the dead." She opened the front cover and breathed in deep through her nose, delighting in the scent of old paper and ink mixed with various spices that must've spilled on the parchment by a previous owner. "I'm hoping to contact my great-grandma Pearl who died last year. She was the coolest lady I ever met."

"It's hard watching our grandparents die of old age," Kody said. "They slow down and can't do the things they loved anymore."

"Oh, no. Getting old didn't kill her. She was harvesting dragon scales from an empty cave when one came back early. She'd forgotten to cast her fire repellent spell." Laney sighed at the ache in her chest that the memory caused. She hoped to be as brave as Grandma Pearl one day. Minus the forgetfulness.

Kody flipped through the pages, pausing occasionally to check out the many hand-drawn illustrations. He stopped at the image of some witches sacrificing a goat. "You have to kill something in order to do a séance?" His face twisted in disgust. "I don't remember reading that on the Ouija Board box. No wonder it never worked."

Laney shut the cover and slid the book back. "That's a more advanced ceremony. I'm obviously not ready for that yet." She slipped the book into her backpack. "I thought it might be fun to learn about."

"Of course. Some people read comic books, you read books about death and sacrifice. We all gotta have hobbies," he said nonchalantly. Kody propped his elbows on the counter. "Anyways, I actually came to ask if you wanted to go to a party with me on Friday."

"Oh. Is it someone's birthday?" Laney loved birthday parties. All the brightly colored decorations and yummy cake. And finding the perfect gift for the birthday person. She loved getting creative with that.

Kody chuckled. "No, it isn't that kind of party." At Laney's frown, he continued. "You know Jennifer Thompson?"

Just the mention of the girl's name caused dread to pool in the pit of her stomach. "Yes, I know her," she said flatly. They had been friends in primary school, up until Jennifer had told the entire class that Laney still wet the bed. One time. One time! She'd drunk too much soda during a sleep-over and had an accident. Laney suspected a spell had also been involved, but she'd never been able to prove it. She hadn't spoken to the girl since.

"Well," Kody said, obviously unaware of the humiliation Laney was reliving in her head. "She's having people over on Friday while her parents are out of town and she asked me to come."

"And you want me to go with you?" She'd never been invited to a high school party before. From what she knew from TV shows and movies, there could be alcohol and drugs, loud music and mayhem. Of course, this could all be exaggerated, like how magic was portrayed. Fear and excitement battled in her gut, leaving her in a cold sweat.

"Yeah," he shrugged. "I still don't know too many people at school, and it would be nice to have a friend with me."

Damn, he'd used the friend card. Kody had only been in Salmagundi a few months. After being attacked by an Eradicator one full moon, he was left with a bum leg, and vulnerable to another attack from the werewolf hunters. His family fled to the magical Alaskan town hidden from the rest of the world for their safety.

Laney glanced around the room, her mind racing to come up with a believable excuse to decline when the large cuckoo clock on the wall caught her attention. It was almost that time. She quickly looked over to the B section of books and gasped. "Hold that thought." She scrambled over to that area. One of the books hadn't been put back properly, its earmuffs sitting next to it on the shelf. Laney held her breath as she slipped the pink, fuzzy earmuffs back on the *History of Banshees* tome, praying she'd been fast enough.

Kody checked his phone. "Oh, shit! Is it six o'clock already?" Before Laney could answer, he covered his ears with his hands, eyes squeezed shut.

A second later, at the top of the hour, a banshee figure flew out of the clock face and shrieked six times. The high-pitched wails echoed off the walls, reverberating throughout the shop. All the books shivered in their spots. If not for the bookstore staff's precautions, the other banshee books would have joined in, making an even greater noise. The stuff of nightmares.

Once the last wail faded away, Kody unplugged his ears. "When is Mrs. Burns going to get that fixed?"

Laney tipped her head from side to side, trying to get the ringing to stop, as she headed back to the front counter. "She's tried every spell she can find. At least it only goes off twice a day now." Laney regrouped the display of feathered quills that had scattered to find refuge. She hoped Kody had forgotten all about Jennifer's party.

"So?" he asked.

Damn, he remembered. She looked at her friend and the puppy dog eyes he was giving her and surrendered. Who could say no to that face? Laney sighed. "Sure, I'll go with you." She had a few days to mentally prepare herself for her first high school party experience. If that was even possible.

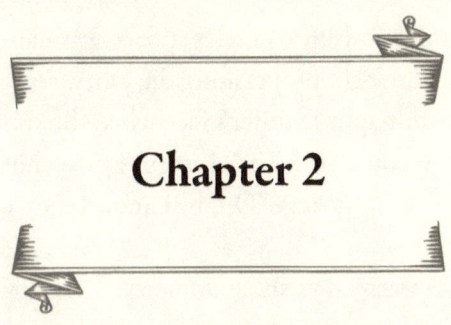

# Chapter 2

"According to the book, *ghosts* are spirits that never crossed over to the Other Realm because they have unfinished business. Most don't even know they're dead." Laney gushed about the new séance book she was reading as she and Kody walked along the sidewalk to the party. When they got to a wooden picket fence, Kody stopped at the little gate and held it open for her.

Laney looked up at the house. Anxiety twisted her stomach and all the excitement about her new book fled. "I'm not sure I'm ready for this." She rubbed her sweaty palm against her hip as she followed Kody up the walkway. Bright, colorful lights spilled out of every window and the loud music pulsed through the ground, sending vibrations up Laney's body, adding to her nerves.

Kody's cane tapped up the steps to the front porch. "We're going to have a great time. And if not, we'll go see a movie or something." He waited until Laney stopped by his side before he leaned closer. "You look nice, by the way."

Laney glanced down at her outfit, pleased that he noticed. "Thanks." Her mom had helped her find the little skirt and sweater. It had taken Laney the better part of an hour to place a warming spell over her legs without causing third degree burns. There were still a few red patches, but only if you looked closely.

"Should we knock or just go in?" he asked. At Laney's shrug, he tapped on the door with the handle of his cane. As the door opened,

Laney stepped closer to him to make sure it was clear that they came together, and she wasn't simply crashing the party.

A wide grin nearly split Jennifer's face when she spotted Kody. "Hey, Kody. I'm glad you could make it." The girl's gaze shifted to Laney, the sparkle in her eyes diminishing. "Oh, hi Laney. I didn't realize you were coming."

Laney's cheeks warmed as she stammered. "Yeah, Kody asked me to come, but if it's a problem, I can leave." She secretly hoped Jennifer would tell her to take a hike. There were so many other things she'd rather be doing tonight. She was only there because of Kody.

He scoffed as he placed a hand at the small of her back and gently encouraged her to enter the house. "Nonsense. There's always room for one more."

Jennifer stepped back to give them room to walk inside. "Of course," she said, smiling brightly at Kody as he passed by. Her smile downright deflated as she glanced at Laney. "The more the merrier," she said sarcastically.

Laney tried to tamp down the eruption of chaotic pixies buzzing in her gut at Jennifer's glare. She must watch her back around the girl. Jennifer probably knew spells that would embarrass her more than simply wetting the bed.

They walked into a huge entryway with a massive, curved staircase. Above them was a gorgeous crystal chandelier that looked like it belonged in an opera house, not a residence. "Nice!" Kody said to Jennifer as he gazed around at all the expensive art hanging on the walls. "Your family must be loaded."

Jennifer giggled. "Yeah, we are." She stumbled and grabbed onto Kody to keep from falling. She kept her hands on his arms to steady herself. "My grandfather invented a potent allergy potion, Sneeze Snuffer, because I'm allergic to cats. He had dozens of the dander-ridden beasts in his lifetime and I couldn't come visit because I'd sneeze myself sick."

Kody pointed to a painting of a man in a business suit and a proud smile surrounded by a bunch of cats. "Is that him?"

"Yep. That's my Grandpa and his furry entourage."

"He had a lot of cats."

Jennifer nodded. "They were a menace to the neighborhood, always harassing the neighbors' dogs and knocking over the trash cans. And that one..." She pointed to the ginger-striped tabby cat with a mangled ear sitting at her grandfather's elbow. "That one hated me. It would put dead rodents on my pillow and was constantly trying to trip me. I wasn't sad when Douglas the Demon Dickhead finally died."

"That's quite the name," Laney said. "I probably would've gone with Fluffy."

Jennifer rolled her eyes and led Kody to the next room. Thumping music and swirling lights filled the air. He reached back and grabbed Laney by the elbow, pulling her along. Someone across the room caught Jennifer's attention and she excused herself, her fingers trailing down Kody's arm as she stepped away.

Laney unclenched her jaw as the girl left. Kody was the first boy to give Laney any positive attention and now Jennifer acted like she wanted to steal him for herself. She hoped Jennifer would too busy with her other guests to remember they were there.

Laney walked with Kody through the crowded room, dodging dancing bodies. He high-fived people and said hello to everyone who greeted him. He seemed pretty popular for someone who didn't know many people yet. Nobody said anything to Laney. Mostly she got confused looks as she followed Kody through the house. She wasn't one for socializing outside of school.

"Hey, Kody! Glad you made it, man," Brian said as he clasped Kody's hand and pulled him into some weird half-hug only guys seem to do.

Kody stepped back and greeted his friend. "Wouldn't miss it. You know Laney, right?"

Laney smiled tightly and gave an awkward wave. "Hey." She'd known *of* Brian for years. He was the captain of the school's hockey team and the star of most high-school girls' romantic fantasies. She'd never actually spoken to him, though.

His forehead creased as his gaze traveled up her body. "Laney? Aren't you the girl who created a rain forest in the cafeteria last year?" He laughed. "Oh, my gawd, the vines. They spread everywhere!" He threw his arms out wide. "They even coiled around some freshman and hung him upside down in the air." His laughter grew as he recalled the events. "Oh! Then the monkeys." He laughed so hard he lost his balance and fell onto a side table. "The monkeys!"

Laney frowned, her cheeks burning as she relived the humiliation all over again. After that incident, nobody had been allowed to work on botany assignments without supervision. Brian struggled to sit upright as he made monkey gestures with his arms. What did girls see in this baboon?

Kody rolled his eyes at the guy and then led her away to another room.

"Why am I here again?" Laney asked as they ran into more people who happily waved at him. "A lack of friends doesn't seem to be an issue for you."

"We're here to have fun."

They ended up in the dining room. Kody made a direct line to the drinks table. A cauldron with red punch bubbled and steamed at the center. Various liquor bottles, half-empty chip bags, and plastic cups littered the rest of the surface. Splashes of punch and greasy dips stained the white tablecloth.

Barry, a guy in Laney's Latin class, bumped into Kody as he approached the table. "Wanna drink, man?" Before getting an answer, he dipped his plastic cup into the cauldron and got a refill. He handed the dripping cup to Kody. "This stuff is amazing."

"Thanks," Kody said, handing the drink back. "This one is yours. I'll get my own."

Barry laughed before downing half the cup in one gulp. He immediately lifted off the floor, bumping his head into the light fixture. "Help a brother out?"

Kody's eyes widened as he gently nudged the guy toward the doorway and watched him float to the next room. "That's so cool."

"Obviously, someone spiked the punch." Laney found a bottle of flat soda and poured herself a cup, hoping it would be safe.

"You don't want to fly?" Kody asked as he ladled himself a cup of punch.

Laney shook her head. "I get air sick."

Kody drank down his cup. As soon as he finished the last drop, he floated to the ceiling. His body sprawled out along the surface as he faced the floor. "This is so weird. Can you hold this?" he asked right before he dropped his cane. Laney caught it and watched her friend flip over and crawl upside down to the next room.

She followed him until she found an empty chair in the living room, out of the way of traffic but still able to keep an eye on Kody. She couldn't shake the feeling of responsibility when it came to him. He was so naïve to magic, and she didn't want him to get hurt. He'd only been in Salmagundi for a few months now, coming from the outside world. If it wasn't for the werewolf that attacked him years ago, he would still be oblivious to magic.

"That's awful," Beverly's voice rang out from the other side of the large plant next to Laney's chair. She was a nice enough girl from school, though a bit of a show-off. Laney couldn't see her through the leaves, or the person she was talking to.

"Yeah. And we can't find a way to break the locking spell he put on it." That was Jennifer. Laney was tempted to sneak away before either girl knew she was listening, but curiosity kept her in her seat.

"What do you think is inside it?" Beverly asked.

Laney leaned in closer, her head practically inside the plant.

"He always told me that the box held his most valuable treasures."

"And he left it to *you* in his will. Not your dad?"

Jennifer didn't respond, so Laney assumed she nodded.

"You could be the richest kid in school," Beverly said.

"I guess we'll never know. Stupid Grandpa," she mumbled the last part. "If only he left instructions on how to open the damn thing."

"Why don't you just ask him?" Laney said out loud. She clapped her hands over her mouth as soon as she realized what she did. Maybe they didn't hear her. Escape was her only option but as soon as she stood to get away, she nearly stumbled into Jennifer. The girl moved quickly. Too quickly. Was she using some sort of super-sonic spell?

"Who are you talking to?" Jennifer asked, arms crossed as she glanced around for anyone else close by.

Heat rushed to Laney's cheeks as she stammered. "No one. I-I was just talking to myself." She tried to step around Jennifer, but the girl blocked her way again.

"Were you eavesdropping on us?" Beverly asked.

Laney groaned. "Kind of. I didn't see you when I sat down. All I know is that you got some locked box you can't open."

"Yeah, from my *dead* grandpa. I can't very well ask him how to open it then, can I?"

Shrugging, Laney said, "Hold a séance." She kept the *duh* inside her head, not wanting to insult the girl and get thrown out of the party without Kody.

Beverly laughed. "Seances are so last century. The school dropped the course decades ago because they couldn't find anyone to teach it."

"Unless you know a local medium," Jennifer added in a taunting tone.

The two friends laughed and turned to go when Laney said, "I can probably do it."

They stopped and turned back to face her. "You know how to contact spirits?" Their doubt in her abilities was crystal clear in their tone. Not that they had much reason to believe in her. Her failures were becoming legendary.

Laney almost let their skepticism erase all the confidence she'd slowly built over the years with every successful spell, but she straightened her shoulders and nodded. "I found a book about it. It actually sounds pretty simple to do. We just need some candles, a white tablecloth, some sweet herbs, and a personal item of the spirit we're trying to reach. There are a few other things mentioned but I don't remember what they are. I gotta look those up."

"Give her a chance," Kody said, standing on the high ceiling above them.

Jennifer and Beverly shared a glance, as if having a telepathic conversation. Beverly glanced at Laney with disgust but after a moment, Jennifer turned back to Laney and nodded. "I'll let you try. But, so help me, if anything goes wrong..."

A hurricane of pixies swirled in Laney's gut. She'd only read through performing a séance one time and now she had to actually contact a spirit. In front of other people, no less. What had she gotten herself into? "It'll be fine."

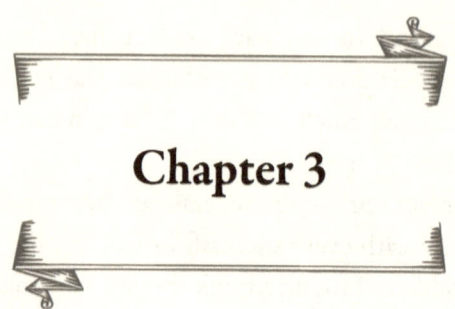

# Chapter 3

"How do I get down? I wanna help contact ghosts," Kody said, floating upside down from the ceiling.

"Did you see the Willy Wonka movie?" Laney asked while she sat back down in the chair. She had given Jennifer a list of items needed for the séance but now she needed to double-check with the book.

"Of course, I saw it. I think Tim Burton did an amazing job. He's one of my favorite film makers. What's your opinion on *The Nightmare Before Christmas*? Do you think it's better than *Corpse Bride*? Personally, I –"

"You need to burp," Laney pulled her backpack off her shoulders. "That's how you get down."

"Oh." Kody belched, descending a few feet. He belched again, this time so loud and long that every conversation in the room halted while all eyes watched him slowly fall back to the floor. Once he was upright and back on his feet, he bowed for the resulting applause. He sat on the arm of Laney's chair, taking back his cane. "Where did that come from?" He motioned to her bag. "You weren't wearing it earlier."

"Sure, I was. I never leave home without my books." She opened her pack and pulled out her latest find. "I put a Notice-Me-Not spell on my bag. I thought it would look strange at a party." She flipped through the pages until she found the chapter she was looking for.

"I think we got what you asked for," Jennifer called from across the room minutes later. "We can do this in the game room. It's the only place with a round table."

Kody stood and held out his hand to help Laney up. She accepted his help but quickly pulled away before he noticed her sweaty palms. They stopped outside the door to the gam room as Jennifer escorted the last guy out. "But I had a royal flush!" he protested.

"Sorry but I need the room. Be right back," she said to Laney as she passed by. A pool table was on one side of the room and the poker table on the other. There was also a locked bar with what looked like expensive bottles of liquor. Stray plastic cups littered every flat surface. Remnants of cigarette smoke lingered in the air, making Laney cough.

Beverly cleared off the poker table, merely moving the dirty cups to the pool table. "Take a seat."

Kody picked up a fallen chair and set it upright for Laney. He sat next to her, leaning his cane against the table between them.

Jennifer came in and set the locked box in the center of the table. It resembled a small treasure chest a pirate might bury in the sand. "This is it."

Laney opened her book and went over the instructions, making sure she remembered everything correctly. She needed to get this right. Failing in front of Jennifer was not an option. "One personal item. Check. Did you have a white tablecloth?"

"Well," Jennifer started, glancing over her shoulder toward the open door. "We have one, but it's currently covered in red punch, vodka and some mysterious, sticky green substance."

Laney pursed her lips as she contemplated whether the tablecloth was vital to the success of reaching the dead grandpa. "The instructions specifically say to use a white tablecloth." The book didn't give a reason why they needed the item, but she really didn't want to use a dirty one. "Do you have a white sheet or towel we could use instead?"

Jennifer snorted. "My mom doesn't do white. The closest we have is my little brother's Spider-Man sheets."

"A fellow Marvel fan." Kody smiled. "Nice."

"It's just a tablecloth, Laney." Jennifer set her hands on her hips as if readying herself for battle. "I'm sure it won't matter if we have it or not."

"But—"

"Any capable witch would be able to do this without the stupid tablecloth," Jennifer said. "Or are we wasting our time? My grandmother used to cast spells perfectly using minor substitutions. But if you don't think you're good enough..."

Laney swallowed down her doubts at the blatant challenge. "No. It's probably not that important. Do we at least have three purple candles?"

Jennifer set a lavender scented three-wick candle on the table. "Does this count as three candles? It's the only purple one I could find."

Laney shrugged. "I...guess? It does have three wicks so...check. Did you find the herbs to burn to sweeten the air like cinnamon or sandalwood?"

Beverly held up a can of air freshener in one hand. "It's apple cinnamon scented." In the other hand, she held up a wooden clog. "I don't know what sandal wood is, but I found this in the mud room."

Laney barely managed *not* rolling her eyes. Getting everything she needed for the séance was proving more difficult than she had originally thought. Jennifer stared at her as if waiting for Laney to buckle. "I guess the air freshener is a check," Laney said and watched Beverly walk around the room, leaving a fall-flavored vapor trail in her wake. She continued down the list. "Do we have some food to entice the spirit to talk with us?"

Jennifer set down a plastic tray with a couple baby carrots and sugar snap peas drowned in room temperature ranch dressing next to the candle. She then shook a crumpled bag of Doritos over the tray, covering it with a few crumbs. "That's all I could wrestle away from the snack table. There might be some leftover shrimp scampi in the fridge but my Grandpa had a shellfish allergy that even his potion couldn't tackle."

"The book doesn't specify the type of food to offer, so the snack food should do. Check." Laney couldn't shake the feeling of doom growing in her gut with every not-quite-right item. She looked through the instructions again. There was a line about needing a gemstone that she hadn't noticed before. Jennifer did have diamond earrings on. That would work. Check. "Let's get started."

The girls joined them at the table, Beverly taking the seat to Laney's left. "Should we light the candles?"

Laney skimmed down the page. "It doesn't say anything about lighting the candles, but perhaps that's assumed? So, yes. Light them up." With the electric lights dimmed and the candles burning, she set the book on the table in front of her and then reached her hands out to her neighbors. Everyone clasped hands.

Laney had to squint to read the print on the page with the low light. She cleared her throat. "Beloved...," She glanced up to Jennifer. "What is your grandpa's name?"

"Marland Edward Oliver Williams."

Kody snickered. "Seriously? With a name like that, no wonder he liked cats."

Jennifer pursed her lips and made it a point not to look in Kody's direction. "Marly was his nickname. Go on, Laney."

Laney nodded and began again. "Beloved Marly. We seek your guidance. We ask that you commune with us and move among us." Laney watched and waited. The book said she would know when she had contacted a spirit by the shift in the air. The temperature would fall yet grow heavier, usually resulting in goosebumps along the medium's skin. The hair along her arms lay perfectly flat.

She repeated the greeting another half-dozen times but nothing out of the ordinary happened. The ticking of the wall clock dominated the silence. Jennifer and Beverly exchanged smirks.

An urgency erupted in Laney's belly. Not wanting to break the connection with the circle, she leaned her head to the table and tried to turn the page with her chin. Three tries and a paper cut later she was reading the next page.

Jennifer pulled her hands away, breaking the circle. "Why am I not surprised it didn't work?" She stood, the legs of her chair scraping along the floor.

Panic rose in Laney's throat, nearly choking her. How was she supposed to succeed if everyone wasn't cooperating? Was Jennifer trying to sabotage her?

"Wait," Kody said before Jennifer could walk off. "We probably just need a goat or live chicken." He leaned closer to Laney and whispered. "Do you need me to find a goat?" The steel glint in his eyes showed he meant business.

His willingness to do whatever she needed to get this right calmed her down a bit. His confidence was exactly what she needed at that moment.

"I hope not." Laney freed her hands and flipped back and forth through the book, looking for more information. Clearly, she was doing something wrong.

"I thought you said you knew how to do this," Beverly said snidely. "I'm not seeing any ghosts."

Embarrassment warmed Laney's cheeks as she searched for the trouble-shooting section of the book. Her chest grew tighter and tighter as their looks of disdain fed her anxiety. Failing in front of Jennifer and Beverly meant the entire school would know before class on Monday. She could already hear the taunts that would be thrown at her as she walked the halls. She wanted nothing more than to shrink into nothingness. A nervous bead of sweat rolled down the center of her back.

"Maybe the box isn't personal enough," suggested Kody. "It's not drawing him in, you know? Do you have anything else? A favorite shirt or maybe a picture of him? Oh, did he wear dentures or a toupee? Can't get more personal than that."

"Not that I think it will help," Jennifer huffed as she walked toward the door. "Hold on." A few moments later she came back in with a white handkerchief balled up in her fist. She plopped it on the table. Inside the rumpled linen sat a gold ring. "Do you think his wedding ring will do?"

"Uh...yeah," Kody said, the duh clear in his tone. "Not as cool as a glass eye would've been, but very personal."

Laney did her best to tamper down the storm of nerves in her gut as she focused on trying again. She picked up the ring and clenched it tightly, concentrating on connecting to the essence of meaning the ring had for this man and using that to reach out to his spirit. Was she strong enough to make this work? Good enough?

"Can we get on with this?" Jennifer interrupted spitefully. "I gotta make sure these people aren't tearing my house apart while we're in here."

Laney set the ring back down on the handkerchief. Once they had created their circle again, she began the welcome sequence. This time she tried to keep Marly more at the forefront of her mind. She was supposed to be the connection between the two worlds. She let the touch of Kody and Beverly's hands keep her grounded in the present while allowing her magic to reach out to the Other Realm. She closed her eyes as she spoke, the weight of the words growing heavier. "Beloved Marly. We seek your guidance."

A gentle tugging sensation in her chest startled her at first, but when Kody tightened his grip, she relaxed and allowed her magic to follow wherever it was being led. Something heavy grabbed onto her magic, like a fish biting a hook. The edge of the table rammed into her ribs as she slid forward in her chair, being pulled forward by her magic. Sweat trickled down her hairline as she reeled back as if boating a marlin.

"Are you okay?" Kody asked.

Laney kept repeating the introduction, not willing to release the hold she had. She was so close. Whether she had successfully reached Marly or someone else, she had no idea, but she didn't want to give up now.

Her hands warmed and tingled as a current ran up her arms. The magic inside her doubled, making it easier to guide the spirit closer. Suddenly, the pulling sensation stopped. Did she lose the connection?

The air cooled, sending a chill down her back. The hair on her arms stood on end.

"Holy shit," Beverly squeaked. "Jennifer, if you're doing that, please stop."

Laney opened her eyes to the sight of a man with short, gray hair and Jennifer's dimple standing next to the girl. He looked like he was trying to pick up the ring but only managed to make it spin on the table. The light from the candle flames flickered over his dark skin, leaving an iridescent aura around him. Her heart pounded. According to the book, visual contact with spirits was rare.

Jennifer stared at the ring with wide eyes. "It's not me."

"Not me either," Kody said as he too couldn't tear his gaze away from the ring. "Is that the spirit?"

Laney frowned. "You can't see him?" He appeared just as solid as any of them.

Jennifer broke the circle and crossed her arms over her chest. "It's probably just Laney trying to make us think she did it. If it really is a spirit, prove it. I know you suck at moving things. Ask the spirit to pick it up."

The man finally managed to get a grip and picked up the ring, raising it about two feet above the table.

"Holy ogre turds," Jennifer breathed. "I think she did it!"

# Chapter 4

"Why didn't they bury me with this?" the ghost of Marly asked as he held his wedding ring in the palm of his hand. He looked toward Jennifer. "It isn't worth anything, my little dragon."

Laney laughed. "Little dragon?"

Jennifer stared at Laney, her face pale. "What did you say?"

Laney's laughter faded as she stammered and motioned with a nod of her head to the ghost standing next to Jennifer. "Th-that's what he just called you. His little dragon." She glanced around at the wrinkled brows of the others. Couldn't they hear him, too?

"Who?" Beverly asked.

The weight of realization pressed upon Laney's shoulders. How could she prove she made contact if no one else could see or hear him? "Her grandpa Marly. He's standing right there."

"They can't hear us or see us," another ghost said as he poked his head between her and Kody, making her jump. "But you can. How curious." An off-white linen covered his head and ears, tying under his beard.

Laney pressed a hand to her chest, willing her heartbeat to return to normal. "Who are you?"

"You just said it was my grandpa." Jennifer whipped her head around, looking for him. "Why can't I see him?"

"That's Marty," a woman said, standing by the pool table wearing a frilly, poofy dress that looked more at home in a royal French garden centuries ago. "I'm Marlene. We weren't sure who you were calling at first but when we realized it was Marly, the two of us tagged along for moral support. He's still new."

"Oh, okay." Laney wasn't sure how to process all this. The book never mentioned emotional support ghosts coming along.

"Okay, what?" Beverly asked. "Are you talking with her grandpa? If so, ask him about the chest."

"I will, but I was just talking to—"

"No! Don't tell them about Marlene and me. Let's not ruin the fun." Marty grinned, exposing his few remaining rotten teeth, and then disappeared. He popped back up by the door. The ghost must've been a beast of a man when he was alive. He had to bend over as he reached for the doorknob. His arm went right through the wood. "Buggar! It's been a while since I've been in the Mortal Realm. Give me a minute."

He stood straight, eyes closed as he reached his arms overhead and pressed his palms together as if praying and then slowly lowered them. Was he meditating?

"Laney!" Jennifer slammed her hand down on the table, stealing back Laney's attention. "Focus. How do I open the box?"

"Oh, right." Laney turned to Marly. "Your granddaughter, Jennifer, would like to know—"

"I heard her," Marly said as he put the ring back down on the table to the gasps of the others watching. "I'm dead, not deaf."

Laney pressed her mouth shut, feeling rightly admonished. "Sorry. This is my first séance."

Marly smiled at her. "That's okay. It's mine, too." He frowned as his gaze drifted to the leftover veggie tray. "I never understood offering food to ghosts who can't even eat it. If that's what that is supposed to be." He then held his hand over the candle, letting the growing flames engulf his fingers. "Doesn't even hurt."

"Holy shit. That's so cool." Kody leaned forward as he watched the flames grow taller.

Marly turned to Marlene. "I thought you said communicating with the living would be harder?"

"It usually is." The older ghost strode over to the table. The large ruffles of her Victorian era dress swooshing across the floor. She bent over and sniffed Laney.

Laney leaned away, not comfortable with such an invasion of personal space. She prayed her deodorant was still working. What clues was the spirit trying to uncover by this?

Marlene straightened; head tilted as she continued to study Laney. "Interesting. I suspect she has a necromancer in her lineage. That would explain why she can see and hear us so easily."

Laney nodded. "Yes. I'm one-sixteenth."

"What—?" Jennifer started.

A squeaking sound echoed throughout the room. Marty had finally figured out how to open the door. He giggled as he swung the door open and closed.

Beverly whimpered. "Make it stop."

"Please stop opening the door?" Laney asked aloud, not confident that Marty would comply because he looked like he was having too much fun.

He vanished again, the door continuing to squeak open and closed on its own. He reappeared by one of the windows and threw them open. A gust of wind came sweeping in and nearly blew out the candles.

They all screamed. Kody was the loudest.

"Stop trying to scare us," Jennifer demanded.

Laney flipped through the pages, searching for any section that could help her control the ghosts. If that was even possible. Maybe she should've finished reading the entire book before she opened her big mouth.

Marty popped up next to her and slammed her book shut, nearly catching her fingers. "Isn't this fun?"

"Laney," Jennifer called in an even voice. "How do I open the box?" Her hands sprawled out flat on top of the table.

"To open the box," Marly started but was stopped by Marlene's hand on his shoulder.

"You can't answer. They didn't include a vital part of the ritual." Marlene frowned at Laney. "Where is the white tablecloth? We simply cannot comply without the white tablecloth."

Laney glared at Jennifer. "*Somebody* convinced me that a white tablecloth wasn't necessary." She faced Marlene. "I'm sorry. Is it really that important?"

The ghost nodded. "It's tradition and simply good manners."

Laney slumped in her seat. Who knew a piece of cloth would be her undoing? She was so close to getting the answers they needed.

Marty appeared on Laney's other side, next to Beverly. "Come on, Marlene. Give the lass a break." He gripped the edge of the table. "Let's show Marly how we have fun. Remember the séance of 1832?"

A smile spread across Marlene's face. "That was rather enjoyable. Fine, but just this once." She stood opposite Marty and held onto her side of the table. Together, they lifted the table off the floor a few inches. Beverly passed out.

"Now this is what I'm talking about!" Kody slid his chair back, away from the floating table. "This is the Best. Séance. Ever!"

"I like this kid," Marty said, looking at Kody. "I want to try him on." He dropped his side of the table.

"What does that mean?" Laney asked, her heart pounding at the gleeful smile on Marty's face. He rushed toward Kody. Was he going to hurt him? Or worse, possess him?

"No!" Laney and Marlene yelled together. Laney leapt out of her seat and threw herself over Kody like a human shield. She had no idea if it would work, but it was the only thing she could think of.

"Whoa! Whatcha doing, Laney?" Kody asked, his arms up by his sides as he looked down at her practically lying across his lap.

"Say no! Say you don't give consent." Laney looked up to the confusion on his face.

The corner of his mouth tipped up as he said, "I actually wouldn't mind if you—"

"Not me! The ghost!" Did he really think Laney was flirting? In front of Jennifer and Beverly?

His eyes widened. "I don't give consent!" He clamped down on Laney's shoulders as his gaze whipped all around the room. "Stay out of me, Mr Ghost!"

Marty stopped next to Kody's chair. "Bugger! It would've been nice to have a body again. Even if just for a moment. I miss," he sniffed. "I miss hugs."

Marlene tried patting the disappointed ghost on the shoulder, but her hand went through him. "Pray thee, behave. Don't ruin Marly's first séance."

Satisfied that Marty wasn't going to jump into Kody's skin, Laney let out a relieved breath. She hadn't gotten to the chapter on possession yet. What if she couldn't convince Marty to get out?

"Why are you on Kody?" Beverly asked, awakening from her earlier bout of fainting. "What did I miss?"

"I was just—"

"Laney! Will you get off him and finish this?" Jennifer shouted. "I still don't know how to open this damn thing." Jennifer motioned to the chest on the table in front of her.

Pushing down the rush of embarrassment flooding her body, Laney climbed off Kody and retook her seat. She wiped her sweaty palms on the front of her skirt as she willed the heat in her cheeks to recede. Kody must've thought she was a total spaz. She cleared her throat. "Marly, can you reveal the way to unlock the box?"

"Is this the box you were speaking of earlier?" Marlene asked Marly.

He smiled. "Yes. It holds many memories."

Laney frowned as she gazed at the box. Jennifer was eager to open it because it was supposed to hold treasure. Did the girl misunderstand what her grandfather meant about the box's contents? Would she blame Laney if whatever was inside couldn't be used on a shopping spree?

"Laney?" Jennifer asked, looking at her expectantly.

There was nothing Laney could do about the contents now. Maybe Jennifer would still be impressed that Laney helped open the box anyway. "Marly?"

"I'm surprised My Little Dragon doesn't remember how to open it. I taught her the spell when she was around eight years old. It's a poem about a little dragon."

"A poem about a little dragon?" Laney asked to clarify. That seemed rather unusual to open a treasure chest.

"A poem about a dragon?" Jennifer repeated. Her expression went blank as if she were deep in thought, trying to dig up the old memory from the dark recesses of her brain.

The door to the game room swung open and a couple guys barged in but then stopped at the sight of the four of them around the poker table. "Oh, sorry. Hey, Kody!" They started howling like wolves.

Kody rolled his eyes. "Not now, guys."

Beverly turned in her chair. "Don't be a punk, Stewart. Get out!"

"Whatever," Stewart grumbled before stumbling down the hall, leaving the door ajar. The music and noise from the remaining partiers drifting into the room.

"The sounds of merriment," Marty said as he perked up. He floated toward the hallway, passing straight through the door. "Come, Marlene. Let's have some fun!"

Marlene hesitated, glancing between the box and the hallway. She sighed and turned to Laney. "Pray thee end the séance before your friend opens the box. If that box contains what I think it does..." She shook her head as she floated out of the room and after Marty.

Laney opened her book again, searching for the instructions on closing the séance. If Marlene was worried, *she* was downright scared. A gemstone was needed to seal shut the portal from the Other Realm, breaking the connection between the two worlds. Laney held out her hand. "Jennifer, I need one of your earrings."

Jennifer unhooked one of diamond studs and handed it over while struggling to remember the words to the poem. "There lived a little dragon...something, something weather? Pleasure? Ugh! Why can't I remember this?"

Laney snatched the diamond earring and quickly uttered the closing phrase. She looked to Marly who was still standing next to his granddaughter, silently encouraging her to remember the words.

"We are most grateful, Marly...and Marty and Marlene, for your visit with us tonight. Please return to the Other Realm in peace and eternal light." Marly didn't budge. Laney repeated the farewell, louder and with more conviction but still the ghost remained.

"Is he gone?" Kody asked, glancing around.

Screams from the other rooms pierced the air. Dread dropped to the bottom of Laney's stomach as Marty's laughter reached her ears.

"I got it!" Jennifer stood and leaned over the box. "There lived a little dragon, whose laughter brought me pleasure, Her love and kindness and her smile, Are my greatest treasure!" A blue light surrounded the box, glowing on her smiling face.

Laney held her breath, gaze locked on the chest. Her pulse raced as she realized she still hadn't closed the séance. The post of Jennifer's earring dug into her palm as she tightened her fist while repeating the chant over and over again under her breath.

A loud click. The lid of the box slowly creaked open, a glowing blue fog spilling out and spreading out over the floor. In moments, it had flowed out under the door and dissipated. Once the box was fully open, Jennifer reached inside.

"Are you kidding me?" She pulled out a handful of pet collars, each with a metal charm and a bell. She dropped them on the table and reached into the chest again. She pulled out a few more and tossed them to the pile. "Please tell me there's more than a bunch of cat stuff."

Kody picked up one of the collars. He examined the charm more closely. "Did your grandpa have a cat named Midnight?" He ran his thumb over the metal. "I think this is gold." He put the charm to his mouth and bit it.

"Well, is it gold?" Beverly asked.

Kody shrugged. "How would I know?"

"Of course, it's not real gold," Marly said. "The treasure is the memories we had with of all my fur babies."

"Yeahhh," Laney said as she watched Jennifer's clenched jaw twitch with every collar and catnip toy she pulled out of the chest. "I don't think she sees it that way."

Jennifer picked up the chest, held it upside down and shook it. More tinkling bells and gold charms clanked on the table along with a square piece of paper. Bits of feather and fluff floated in the air.

Beverly picked up the paper before Jennifer slammed the box back down on the table. "Is this you and Marly?" She handed it to the furious red-faced girl.

Jennifer snatched the photo from her hand. As soon as she glanced at the picture, she sucked in a breath. "Oh." After a few moments of staring at the photo, a single tear ran down her cheek. She fell back into her chair. "I miss him."

Marly placed a hand on her shoulder. Or...through her shoulder. "I miss you too, Little Dragon."

Laney's eyes stung as she watched. Everything in the chest seemed harmless. They must've avoided whatever Marlene was worried about.

Stewart came running into the room, out of breath. "Jennifer! There is a...situation out here you should probably see."

Or maybe not.

# Chapter 5

Jennifer swiped the moisture from her eyes before jumping to her feet. "What now? Can't you see I'm having a moment?" She stomped out of the room, following Stewart down the hall.

Beverly leaned back in her chair, staring at the poker table. "I can't believe you did it, Laney. You actually contacted a ghost and helped Jennifer open the box. I'm impressed."

Pride swelled in Laney's chest at the girl's words. She wasn't used to impressing anybody.

"Of course, she did it." Kody picked up his cane from where it had fallen on the floor. "I told you she would."

Beverly stood. "I'm going to go help Jennifer clean up whatever situation is out there. We're done here, right?"

Laney bit the inside of her lip as she contemplated whether or not to be totally up front with the current situation. "Um, yeah. Kody and I can take care of this room."

"Great." Beverly turned up the lights on her way out.

Kody leaned on his cane as he stood. "That was awesome. Should we blow out the candles and clean off the table?"

Laney barely heard him as she reread the instructions on ending the séance. Why wasn't it working? Marly floated over and read over her shoulder. "Do you think the lack of the tablecloth is keeping me here?" he asked.

"I don't know." She recited the words correctly. She had a gemstone. What was she missing?

"I'll clean up anyway," Kody said, dropping the cat collars back into the chest. "I can't believe her grandpa wanted to possess me. That's wild."

"No, that was Marty." Laney checked to make sure that there wasn't a missing page or that two pages hadn't stuck together.

"Who's Marty?"

Laney looked up from the book. She forgot that she hadn't told anybody about the other two. "He's one of Marly's support ghosts. He and Marlene are probably the situation that Jennifer is dealing with. If only I could close out this séance."

Kody glanced around the room. "You mean the ghosts are still here?"

"Laney!" Jennifer screamed from the other room. Footsteps grew louder until the door slammed open. "Please explain why things are flying all over the place, including some of my guests." She stood in the doorway, hands on her hips and glaring at Laney.

"Why is this her fault?" Kody asked. "You're having a party with a houseful of drunk witches. I'm surprised you're not overrun with frogs by now." He waved his cane around and then pointed it at Laney. "Poof! You're a frog."

"Transfiguration is actually very difficult to do when sober," Laney explained. "Let alone drunk. Drugs generally impair magical abilities."

"Exactly," Jennifer said. "People are freaking out and running out of here, screaming. And since you're the only sober witch in the house..."

"Maybe we should go see what's going on," Marly suggested. "Marlene might be able to help close the séance." He didn't wait for Laney as he floated through Jennifer on his way out.

Jennifer shivered and then glanced up at the air vent. "Did the AC kick on?"

Laney stood abruptly, nearing knocking over her chair. "Let's go check this out." She clutched the book to her chest as she marched to the other room. The click of Kody's cane on the hardwood floor followed her.

About a dozen kids remained in the living room, each crying or screaming at something. Marty and Marlene sat on the fireplace mantal, laughing at a kid spinning in a circle like a dog chasing its tail. At first, Laney couldn't see what was distressing the guy as he kept reaching behind him. Then she noticed an orange, fuzzy lump in the center of his back. And a tail whipping by.

"Is that...?" She stopped the kid, bracing his shoulders so he wouldn't fall over, and glanced at his back. An orange tabby cat had clawed onto the kid's shirt. She reached out to detach the cat but couldn't touch it. Her hands went right through it.

"Get it off!" the kid cried.

"Ummm..." Laney looked to Marlene on the mantal. "How do I fix this?"

All around the room, Laney began noticing cats all over the place. A couple cats looked to be racing down the drapes, shredding the fabric on the way down. A Siamese cat kept swatting at some girl's ponytail. Another was pulling on the tablecloth in the dining room, spilling everything onto the floor with a big crash.

A girl ran down the stairs screaming. "The toilet paper is possessed!"

Glass shattered on the kitchen floor. Laney followed Jennifer to investigate. Sitting on the draining board was a short-haired black cat looking on the floor at the broken bottle. When it saw the girls in the doorway, it strolled over to a dirty glass and casually knocked it off the counter too.

Jennifer gasped. "What is going on? Why are the glasses jumping to their deaths? Is my grandfather's ghost making all this mess? Terrorizing people?"

"Not your grandpa," Laney said. "But I think his cats are. I think they were in the chest you opened."

"Are you saying this is all my fault?" Jennifer spun around and got right into Laney's face. "You're the one who brought these ghosts here. You better find a way to make them go away."

Laney's heart pounded as humiliation loomed large. "I'm trying, but for some reason it isn't working. I recited the ending chant while holding your diamond but..." She shrugged and opened her hand to show the girl the diamond earring she borrowed for the spell.

Jennifer picked up her earring. "That's because this isn't a diamond. It's a cubic zirconia. Jason couldn't afford real diamonds but he's hot, so I let him give these to me."

Laney couldn't help the smile that spread across her face. The problem wasn't with her, but her tools. Something easily fixed. "Do you have any genuine diamonds or any other gemstone I could use?" Her pulsed raced knowing she was seconds away from clearing up the whole mess.

"Is that all you need?" At Laney's nod, Jennifer marched away, muttering something unpleasant about Laney's intelligence under her breath.

Kody nearly ran into Jennifer as he walked into the kitchen. "Did that Marty ghost do all this?" He motioned to the broken glass on the floor and to the general scattering of dirty napkins, paper plates, and half-empty plastic cups on every flat surface.

"No. We have an infestation of cat ghosts that we are minutes away from shooing off. Jennifer's getting me a real gemstone."

Marlene, Marty, and Marly floated through the refrigerator and into the kitchen. "Ah, Laney. There you are," Marlene said. "We are most grateful for the invitation to your séance, even if you didn't intend on a couple extra guests. But we must be on our way. We cannot stay in this realm for too long."

"Why is that?" Laney asked.

"We could get trapped here." Marty shrugged. "This realm is fun to visit from time to time, but the Other Realm is so much nicer. At least for us spirits."

"Okay," Laney said. "Jennifer should be right back with the gemstone. Then I can send you and the cats back to the Other Realm."

"Are you talking to the ghosts right now?" Kody asked, looking at the refrigerator since that was the same direction that Laney faced. In a much louder voice he said, "It was nice meeting you."

Marty laughed. "I love this kid!"

"Indeed." Marlene smiled gently at Laney. "We will be on our way."

"Thank you," Marly said. "I'm glad my Little Dragon has a friend like you." He reached down and tried to pat the head of one of the cats that kept passing through his leg.

The three ghosts began to fade away.

"Wait!" Laney called out. "Don't I need to close out the séance for you to go back?"

"Nonsense," Marlene said, looking more like a ghost than she did before. "That is simply a formality created by the living to make them feel in charge. Farewell, my friend. I'm sure we will see you again."

"But what about the cats? Aren't you going to take them with you?" A black and gray striped cat had knocked over a roll of paper towels and was currently unrolling it down the center of the kitchen.

"We can try." Marlene patted her legs as she called out. "Here kitty, kitty."

Marly had more success as he kneeled and pursed his lips with a "psss, psss, psss." Most of the cats ran straight to him. A couple were too busy cleaning themselves to notice anything else.

Laney ran over to those cats and shooed them over to the ghosts. "Time to go home now." She used some kitchen twine to lure another to the waiting group.

After about ten minutes of herding cats, Laney stopped to count. "It looks like thirteen. No, fourteen. Wait." She recounted again. "Thirteen."

"I think that's all of them." Marly smiled at his furry friends. "Thanks again, Laney."

A moment later, they all started to fade away when Marlene spoke up. "Don't forget to close the—"

"Laney!"

Laney dashed into the living room to see Jennifer standing in front of the fireplace, holding up the remains of a porcelain figurine of a dog. "Send those ghosts back before they totally destroy my house."

Laney glanced into the kitchen to find the cats had vanished. "They already left. And the ghosts aren't responsible for *all* this mess."

Jennifer glared as she set the broken pieces on the mantal. "Whatever." She held up a diamond necklace. "Will this do?"

"Oh, uh... yeah." Laney thought Marlene said that closing the séance was just a formality but then she reminded Laney to close it as she was fading away. She took the necklace from Jennifer anyway and recited the closing chant, again. Then handed it back.

Jennifer slipped the necklace into her pocket. "Well. Thanks for helping me open my chest. I guess you're not totally useless." She strolled over to Kody and slipped her arm around his. "I don't suppose you'd want to stay and help me clean up? I'm sure Laney can see herself home."

Laney wanted to gag at the sight of Jennifer fawning all over Kody. But she couldn't help but notice how cute they looked together. Did he want to stay and help her? Was Laney being a third wheel? "I can let myself out."

She spun around so she didn't have to look at them anymore and marched straight to the front door. Rejection squeezed her chest. She reminded herself that Kody was her friend, and she wanted her friend to be happy.

"Wait up," he called out. "You're breaking rule number one. Always leave with the one you came with." He opened the front door and held it open for her. As she passed by, he leaned closer and whispered. "I can't believe you were going to leave me alone with her. She's kinda scary."

Laney laughed, feeling like she was floating beside him as they walked to the sidewalk.

Then Laney came to an abrupt stop at the sight of an orange tabby cat with a mangled ear sitting on the wood fence. It stared at her, flicking its tail defiantly. A moment later, more cats hopped up on the fence and sat in a line, all staring at her. Twelve in all.

All heat drained from Laney's body, making her shiver.

"What's wrong?" Kody waited, holding the little gate open for her.

"How many cats did Jennifer say her grandpa had?" Laney had counted thirteen cats. Was that not all of them?

Kody shrugged. "Dozens, I think she said. Why?"

And then as if they had coordinated their exit, all the cats turned and jumped from the fence and scattered down the street. Out of sight. Moments later, a woman's scream pierced the night.

Dread sat like a rock in the pit of Laney's stomach. What had she unleashed to the unsuspecting town of Salmagundi? "I think we might need to find a goat."

Meanwhile, back in the Other Realm...

"Don't forget to close the box," Marlene called out to Laney as she and the other ghosts transitioned to their home realm. They ended up in the same house they had just left, only it was void of living people.

"Why does she need to close the box," Marty asked. He tried to pick up one of the cats, but his hands went straight through it.

"I am assuming that the cats came into the Mortal Realm through the box," she said as she strolled out of the house.

A half man/troll wandered down the street, his face scrunched up in confusion. Marly waved. "Hi Randy."

Marlene continued. "The box must be a portal. Unless Laney wants to be bothered by more ghosts or worse, she would do well to close and seal that box."

"I'm sure she'll follow your instruction," Marly said as he followed his friends to the gate to see them out. "She's a bright, young necromancer."

**Acknowledgements**

Publishing a book is a long process that takes many people to bring the dream to life. I'd like to thank Kat, Cheryl, Kelly, Mason, Gillian, and the Stonehenge writers' group for the honest and helpful critiques and the brainstorming sessions that helped create this fun little story.

**About the Author**

**R.A. Gates** – R. A. is a single, working mom living in Sacramento, CA. But you can call her Ruth. She enjoys writing what she loves reading most which is young adult, urban fantasy. She loves writing about strong characters that may not realize just how strong they actually are. Humor is also part of her writing because she can't help it. She never matured past sixteen.

Go to Ruth's website, ragates.wordpress.com to find out more about her and what she's currently writing.

Do you want to know how Laney and Kody met? Sign up for my newsletter and get the ebook, The Tenth Life of Mr. Whiskers as a thank you.

Scan me!

**Also by this Author**

### The Tenth Life of Mr. Whiskers

Mr. Whiskers is dead—muerto—shuffled off his mortal coil. All Laney had to do was watch the store and feed the cat. Too bad she hadn't known there was a cat. She has a plan, though. An obscure spell contains the power to grant life, only long enough to save her job, and her vacation in Paris. Just because she botches the simplest of spells doesn't mean she can't control complicated magic, right? The mysterious new guy at school, Kody, goes along for the ride; providing emotional support and, well, let's be honest, he's just hot. After struggling through the spell—when nothing seems to be going right—they find that giving Mr. Whiskers a tenth life turns out to be more than they bargained for.

**Fragments of Darkness: An Anthology of Thrilling Stories**

From between the cracks of imagination, among the splinters of the unknown, and upon the winds of mystery, lurk the Fragments of Darkness. With legends of killer mermaids to tales of Civil War era ghosts, ten passionate story-tellers come together to bring you yarns of fantasy, paranormal, and chills and thrills that will entertain, intrigue, and enchant young adult and new adult readers. Stories included in this anthology: Dorothy Dreyer - Under the Surface; C.L. Campbell – Reckoner; Lisa M. Basso - Heart and Bone; Pat Esden - Black as a Dark Moon, Scarlet as Sumac; E.M. Fitch - Between Shadows; R.A. Gates - The Collector; Jessica Gunn - The Ghost; Debra Jess - Blood & Armor; Melanie McFarlane - The Transgressions of Faithe Eileen; Daphne René - Story of the Unknown Soldier

**The Servants and the Beast: In which the ones who saw it all tell the true tale of the Beast**

You think you know the story – prince gets cursed, girl meets Beast, they fall in love and live happily ever after. If only it was that simple. But dating is tough even in the best of circumstances. Ever since the fateful day when we let that horrible Good Fairy into the castle, our lives have been on hold. When she turned our bad-tempered prince into a Beast, she lumped us, his loyal servants, into the curse too, just because she assumed his rude behavior was our fault. Theodore the butler should never have let her inside, and the rest of us should have helped bar the door. Now, Theodore is an armchair, and we're all trying to carry on our duties as a piano, a coat rack, a bookcase and the like. At least we have Robert to clean up the pink sparkles piling in the corners from the Good Fairy's curse, since he's a mop now. We know we just need the Beast to fall in love to break the spell. We're all doing whatever we can to help him find True Love, one visitor at a time, hoping the right person finally comes along—but will the Beast ever learn to love?

**After the Sparkles Settled: In which the ones who survived the curse celebrate Christmas**

The five authors who collaborated for The Servants and the Beast have come together again to bring you this very special Christmas tale, looking in on the characters at the castle several months after the curse was lifted. As they celebrate the holidays, you can find out what's happened to your favorite characters. Is Hugo finally courting Isadora? Has Quillsby learned to keep a secret? Will Robert propose to Lady Jayne—or Charles to Frostine? And how are Estienne and Beau doing, now that the Beast is a Prince again? Enjoy this Christmas epilogue to The Servants and the Beast.

**Plot Twists: or Into the Pages**

Down forgotten alleyways and quiet streets, mysterious bookstores only reveal themselves to people who need the special volumes on their shelves. People who are lonely, people who are lost, or people who want an unforgettable experience, find themselves inexplicably drawn to particular works. The keepers of the book, just as strange as the stores themselves, will ask:

*"Where would you venture inside the Phantom's Opera?"*
*"Have you dreamed of sitting at Arthur's Round Table?"*
*"Would you dare to meet Frankenstein?"*

Follow nine authors as they weave tales of characters finding exactly what they need, expected or not, inside the pages of a book. With stories across the ages explored: from the heroes of the Iliad, to the madness of Alice's Wonderland, to the horror of H.P. Lovecraft, adventure awaits.

## Pesto and Potions

Modern Love - Ancient Foes

With vampires on the rise and the city under threat, who would have thought love – and a long lost recipe for pesto - could bring everything undead to a head?

Lola Morelli enjoys her life in Sacramento - jumping over walls with her parkour team during the day and climbing the kitchen ladder to be head chef at the hottest restaurant at night. Even her love life is going great. She doesn't have one special woman in her life, she has several. Sure, she's concerned about all the stories of the Disappeared, but the rise of missing people isn't enough for her to change her ways.

Charlie Ryan has a lot on her shoulders - dancing as a professional ballerina, grieving the loss of her grandparents, and facing pressure from her fellow witches to help with the growing vampire menace. It's a lot for one woman to handle. But life starts looking up when she meets the attractive chef at her new favorite restaurant, and not just because she can make an amazing vegan dish or keep up with Charlie at a Pilates class.

With the number of Disappeared growing, Charlie's coven is desperate to protect the people of Sacramento. It isn't until Charlie meets Lola that the witches find a delicious secret weapon that could tip the balance against the bloodsuckers. But will Lola understand that Charlie's not just into her because of her pesto recipe? Can Lola and Charlie's new spark of romance withstand the secrets and lies needed to keep everyone safe?

**Pucker Up**

Ivy always thought that breaking a curse with True Love's Kiss was the ultimate romantic gesture in fairy tales. But when she has to plant one on a prince who's been dead for 200 years, it's just gross.

After the "incident", seventeen-year-old Ivy discovers she's a witch, and she's not at all happy about it. An underground organization of human warriors called the Eradicators are hunting her, like they do all other creatures tainted with magic—witches and wizards, werewolves, vampires, and fae to name a few. To escape, she's found refuge in Salmagundi; a town hidden behind magical wards to anyone who doesn't use magic.

But she can't relax yet. The secret she keeps about her past could get her killed if discovered. Keeping a low profile is her main goal. Too bad Garren—the most obnoxious, pretentious, and not hot guy she ever met—won't leave her alone. No other person on the planet can get her blood racing like he can.

Now the wards are failing, putting every resident in danger of being discovered by the Eradicators.

Thankfully, a possible solution has been found, and Ivy is the key. All she has to do is awaken the wizard prince who cast the wards over 200 years ago and bring him back to Salmagundi to save the town. Only two obstacles stand in the way: his whereabouts are unknown and only True Love's Kiss can break the curse he's under.

That's right. She has to kiss the dead guy!

Together with her cousin and tag-a-long Garren, she sets out on a quest to find her prince. After putting up with dragons, vampires and one too many necrophilia jokes, can she survive long enough to take one for the team and PUCKER UP?

**Bonus #1**

**A short story written from the prompt "You had one job to do."**

"You had one job to do," Mrs. Renfield told Laney as she pinched the bridge of her nose. "The simplest job I could find. The one job I thought couldn't end in disaster. But leave it to you to find a way to mess it up."

Laney stared at the ground below her feet, waiting for her high school Charms teacher's rant to end. She was totally overreacting. Laney did exactly what she was told to do. She just added a little extra pizzazz, that's all. It was the school's biggest fall event after all; the Autumn Carnival. Her booth had to compete with the big rides and games. No one was stopping by her booth.

"Everyone is in a panic! Parents are threatening to sue the school. Arthur!" Mrs. Renfield pointed across the parking lot where the carnival was set up. Arthur ran to where she pointed with his magical cloud safety net and made it just in time to catch the child falling from the sky. Most of the teachers were busy catching falling children all over the carnival.

Mrs. Renfield sighed, one hand over her chest. She turned to Laney and exploded. "What were you thinking?"

Laney waited a second to answer, just in case she wasn't finished. At the raise of her teacher's eyebrow, Laney said, "The helium tank you gave me was almost empty and –"

"Then why didn't you tell me?" Mrs. Renfield asked. "I have another tank in the supply closet."

"You were busy charming all the scarecrows to dance around the fair. I didn't want to bother you so I figured I could just use a spell to inflate the balloons."

"Of course, you did," her teacher said. "What spell did you use?"

"A Mary Poppins spell. I found it in a new spell book that came into the bookstore." Laney worked at the local bookstore and had access to the latest editions. This particular book had all sorts of Disney themed spells and enchantments.

"This is amazing!!" Came a voice directly above them. Laney glanced up to see her friend, Kody, flying in the air while holding on to a bright red balloon. Laughter and excited squeals filled the air as dozens of children of all ages floated above the town, a few drifting off into the woods. The parents, on the other hand, were running into each other as the shouted and chased after their airborne children, trying to stay beneath them if they let go of the string and fell. It was utter chaos.

Mrs. Renfield glared at Laney. "Please don't volunteer to help with another school function. I don't think the school can afford it."

Bonus #2

## Chapter 1 of Pucker Up

"What are you doing out here?" Ivy asked her young friend sitting on the back steps of the boarding house. The wooden gate slammed shut behind her as she strolled through the back garden, her skateboard in hand.

Danny didn't answer. His body shivered underneath his jacket, zipped all the way to his chin to keep out the April breeze. Being the youngest werewolf in Salmagundi, he recovered slowly after the regular transformations and the last full moon was only two days ago. She was thankful that the only monthly transformation she had to deal with was of the PMS variety.

Black Converse crunched on the gravel path leading to the back patio. She slid her overflowing backpack off her shoulder and dropped it onto the patio steps, cracking one of the old planks. She stretched the kinks out of her back.

*Death by homework,* she thought.

Scooting Danny over, she sat next to him. The late afternoon sun hung over the mountains surrounding the Southeastern Alaska town, casting long shadows on the ground.

The orphan boy's hands trembled as he petted Lieutenant Dan, the local three-legged stray cat. Danny brushed strands of blond hair out of his eyes and looked up at her. "I'm in big trouble, Ivy. He's gonna kill me this time, for sure."

At first, she dismissed his dramatics as typical ten-year-old behavior, but then tears threatened to fall from his large, blue eyes and her heart dropped into her gut.

"What happened?"

"You know that antique rug in the parlor?"

"Yeah."

"Well, Athena said Mr. McGregor sold it today, to some dealer in Washington he's visiting this weekend." He stopped petting the cat and wiped his sweaty palms on his pants. "The thing is, about a month ago, I accidentally spilled grape juice on it and hid the stain under the chair, so he wouldn't see it."

He was right. Danny was going to die when his foster dad found out. She'd seen her penny-pinching landlord's temper flare, especially after a few drinks. And being a werewolf didn't soften his disposition, either.

"Has he found it yet?"

"I don't think so, but he's gonna see it when he moves the chair and then I'm a dead man."

"What did Athena say to do?" She assumed he told the boarding house's only other tenant about his problem, considering he worshipped the ground she walked on. What was so great about Athena anyway? She was merely a narcissistic bitch who used her big boobs and Hollywood smile to charm her way into, or out of, any situation.

"She said, 'Sucks to be you' and left for her date."

*Yep, that sounds about right.*

"Danny!" They both jumped when Mr. McGregor's voice boomed through the house and rattled the kitchen window above them.

Danny's whole body shook as he moaned into his hands. He had never gotten into any real trouble with Mr. McGregor because everything always seemed to be blamed on her. Even though she was fearful for Danny, a small part of her looked forward to seeing someone else get punished for a change.

"Come on. He'll just get madder if he has to come looking for you." She nudged his elbow and stood. Pausing at the screen door, she waited for him to follow.

He reluctantly dragged his shoes along the scuffed wooden floor of the old Victorian house towards the scene of the crime. On the way, he mumbled a little prayer to spare his life. *Talk about overreacting.* But when they entered the room, Mr. McGregor's cold, dark eyes narrowed into slits as they homed in on Danny.

*Or, maybe not.*

Every line etched in the older man's face from decades of harsh transformations deepened under his scowl. His chest rose and fell with each controlled breath. "Do ye have something to tell, laddie?" His Scottish brogue was low and slurred, but the anger was loud and clear.

Danny froze. His eyes grew wide and his face paled two shades. He looked like he was going to throw up. Swallowing hard, he raised his chin to look Mr. McGregor in the eye and said, "Ivy did it."

*That little shit!* She opened her mouth to set the record straight, but by the way his legs shook in his jeans, she couldn't do it.

Throwing a glare at the little liar, she faced Mr. McGregor. "Yeah, I ruined the rug, sir. I was running late for work, so I covered it up thinking I'd clean it later. I must've forgotten about it. Sorry." She stood there, completely still, trying not to set off his hair trigger temper bubbling under the surface. Even breathing too loud seemed risky as she waited for him to speak.

Mr. McGregor regarded them both for a few moments, one bushy eyebrow raised, before uttering a word. "Danny, go to yer room, and shut the door behind ye."

Danny glanced at her, uncertainty in his eyes.

*Oh sure, now you worry about me. Where was the concern when you threw me under the bus?* She nodded her head, keeping her thoughts to herself. He stepped away, watching her until he disappeared around the corner.

Mr. McGregor loomed before her, like a bull before a matador, staring her down. His scotch-soaked breath hung in the air between them like a toxic cloud. She had to close her mouth to keep from gagging.

"Ye did this?"

Her eyes followed his meaty finger pointing to a large purple spot on the very beautiful but very *ruined* Oriental rug. She expected to see a spot about the size of a dinner plate, at the most. But no, Danny must have spilled the entire bottle of juice to get a stain so large. It was at least two feet across. "Yes, sir."

He stood there, staring. The vein at his temple throbbed close to the point of bursting and his worn face was so red, he looked like he'd have a heart attack right in front of her.

She'd met younger, stronger werewolves in the past, but there was a feral glint in his eyes that twisted her stomach. Her fingers twitched, eager to grab the silver stake she would normally keep on her belt. Too bad it remained hidden in her backpack on the porch. Silver wasn't allowed in the boarding house.

"Are ye trying to make me look the fool? Do ye think I don't know the boy did this?" Foam gathered at the corner of his mouth as the tone of his voice took on a dangerous growl.

Her body tensed as adrenaline sped to every muscle, preparing to put her childhood years of combat training to use. Or at least she hoped. It had been over a year since her last fight and she was rusty.

His nostrils flared with each restrained breath as he waited for her reply. Should she stick to the lie or fess up? Deciding that a noncommittal, middle ground was her best bet, she shrugged.

Suddenly, air heaved from her lungs as her body was slammed backwards into the wall. Being drunk hadn't slowed him down at all. A dense fog invaded her brain, shutting down any coherent thought. When the fuzz cleared a moment later, she became aware of his forearm crushing against her windpipe and her right wrist was pinned above her head. Fear flared up inside her when repeated attempts to draw more than a trickle of air proved impossible.

*Don't panic, don't submit.* That's what he wanted. Gathering courage, she pushed down the hysteria that sloshed at her calves like a rising tide, threatening to swallow her whole. She defiantly maintained eye contact with the crazed man, daring to call his bluff.

"Ye think that 'cause yer a witch, ye can disrespect me?" He leaned forward, pressing into her throat even more. "I will not be lied to in my own home."

An excruciating minute passed before she succumbed to the panic she bravely fought off. Frantic fingers clawed at his face. Too bad she had already gnawed all her nails down to stubs. Changing tactics, she pushed the heel of her free hand at his chin, stretching his neck. Her hand slipped when he wretched his head sideways and the side of her wrist scraped across his teeth, nicking the skin. How much longer could she hold out?

She punched and kicked at any and every part of him. Then, a warm buzz, like a hive of angry bees, swelled inside her. Her magic ached to explode and end her torment. Gathering the will to ignore her choking, she placed her palms on his chest and released all the pent-up magic in one blow. Power jolted from her hands like shock paddles and slammed into the angry Scot, sending him and anything not bolted down flying across the room. He hit the wall with a loud crack and slumped to the floor.

Ivy collapsed, trembling and sucking air into her burning lungs. Books and loose papers coated the floor and the easy chair hiding the stain lay toppled on its side. Broken glass from fallen picture frames littered the edges of the room. A groan from across the parlor quickened her pulse.

*That's my cue to leave.* She scrambled to the open doorway as best she could. Using so much magic drained most of her energy, but she willed her rubber legs to move. Werewolves were a sturdy bunch and it was going to take a lot more than crashing against a wall to keep him down.

Heavy footsteps shook the floor as they grew closer. She pulled herself to her feet using the door frame and staggered into the hall. But before she was clear of the room, a strong hand clamped down on the back of her neck and pulled her backwards. She bit back a scream while attempting to tear off the fleshy hook.

His nails dug into her skin as he forced her body down, bending her at the waist in front of him.

She whimpered.

He held her there for at least a hundred ticks of the grandfather clock as she stared at the dried mud splattered across the toes of his boots.

"Ye owe me five thousand dollars," he said in a raspy voice, his grip tightening. "One month ye have, or both you and the boy are out on the street."

"You can't do that," she croaked. "No one else will take in a young werewolf." Images of Danny huddled in a cardboard box in an alley flashed before her eyes.

"Try me." He released her with a final shove to the floor and walked away without another word.

She waited face down on the dirty hardwood floor until she heard a door slam upstairs. She propped herself up on her elbows and sighed. *Great. Now I owe Mr. McGregor money I don't have.* Even if she worked extra shifts at the diner, and kissed major butt for tips, she still couldn't make enough in time.

"Are you all right?" Danny cowered in the doorway watching her struggle to her feet.

"Well, I'm alive." She rubbed the back of her neck as she hobbled past him. Brushing the dust off her jeans, she lumbered outside to retrieve her book bag and skateboard when the phone rang. The odds that it was for her were slim, so she trod upstairs to drink a healing potion for her throat and get started on the hours of homework waiting for her.

Just as she opened her bedroom door, Danny yelled out. "Ivy, it's for you."

"Take a message." It was Friday. She was tired and felt like a wrung-out rag. The last thing she wanted to do was be guilted into working a late-night shift at the diner tonight, even though she could really use the money. She trudged to the bathroom down the hall and then chugged down the last bottle of healing potion. The bitter taste lingered on her tongue as the liquid soothed her throat. The strengthening potion smelled like feet, but she swallowed that down, too, instantly perking up. Medicine, magical or not, always tasted awful.

Closing the cabinet, she caught her reflection in the mirror. Underneath her dark curls, the red marks on the sides of her neck from Mr. McGregor's fingers glared at her. He'd surprised her with his speed as much as she surprised herself with her sluggishness. She foresaw grueling hours of training to get back in shape in her future.

Unshed tears prickled her eyes as she stared at the little marks, reminders of how she let her fear take over. She was reckless, careless to let the situation get so out of control. A year ago, she would've had him on the floor, begging for mercy. Of course, a year ago her entire life was different: her mother was still alive, and she wasn't cursed with magical powers. Now she was hunted outside Salmagundi's borders. She squeezed her eyes shut, pushing back the tears that begged for release.

Maybe all that's happened was some sort of cosmic punishment for what she used to be, used to do. All of her past prejudices and bad choices haunted her now. She couldn't keep living with these ghosts constantly eating at her soul and robbing her of any happiness. If only there was a way to make up for her past.

After a few calming breaths, she forced her emotions back down where they belonged. She grabbed a wad of toilet paper and blew her nose. From this moment forward, she was determined to redeem herself, somehow.

As she washed her hands, a small cut on her wrist stung under the cold water. His teeth were sharp for not even being a full moon. She froze.

He bit her. Indirectly, but his teeth still punctured her skin. And his saliva, with all its germs and magic, could've contaminated her blood.

*Crap. Karma strikes again.*

A moment later, rationale took over and she realized that she couldn't become a werewolf because she was already a witch. The two different magics couldn't live inside the same person. *Duh.* One always dominated the other and because she was born a witch, she'd stay a witch. At least she'd be spared the anguish of fleas.

Danny sat on the floor, leaning against the wall across from the bathroom when she came out. "Your cousin Thing called."

"You mean Thane?"

"Yeah, that's what I said. He needs to talk to you 'bout something important. He wants you to come over to his house right away." He scrambled to his feet.

She held in a groan. Thane was a fellow Senior at school and a nice enough guy, though a bit high strung. He discovered a lost letter in his late uncle's trunk that her mother had written when she was pregnant with her. Her father, Thane's uncle, died before telling anyone he was a new dad, so nobody in Thane's— and now her—family knew she even existed until three days ago.

The last couple of days had been hell for her with Thane following her around asking a million questions to 'get to know her better'. They'd had casual conversations in the past, usually homework related, but now he wouldn't shut up. She couldn't take it anymore.

"I'm sure whatever he wants to talk about can wait until Monday." She pushed past her bedroom door and headed to the desk to pull out her Trigonometry homework.

"But," Danny said as he barged in. "He told me he'd give me ten bucks if I get you to go over there."

She stopped. "He did?" How badly did he want to know about her childhood pets, or where she went on vacation?

"Yeah, so go."

Sitting in her chair, she looked Danny over from head to toe. For once, he might be useful to her. "Is Garren going to be there?"

"Who?"

"Never mind." She twisted the wide leather bracelet that never left her right wrist as she thought. "Tell you what. I'll go if you donate Thane's bribe money to the New Rug Fund."

"What?" His voice screeched out a high note. His eyes grew so wide that the whites were visible all around his irises.

"You're the one who ruined the rug in the first place, remember? Besides, do you want to go back to the orphanage that kept you locked in a cage like a dog?"

He froze in his step, terror reflected in his eyes. "I don't wanna go back there."

Mr. McGregor may be son of a bitch, but at least he treated Danny like a human being. No cages for werewolves in his house.

"If we don't come up with $5,000 soon, we're both outta here."

His shoulders sagged as he dropped his gaze to the floor. "Fine."

She grabbed her hoodie and skateboard. "You should've asked for twenty."

"Hey, Ivy?"

She stopped with her hand on the doorknob and waited.

"If you have a cousin, does that mean you're going to move out and live with him now?"

Her heart cracked at the tremor in his voice. "I'm not going anywhere."

He smiled.

"All right, out. I have to go earn our first ten dollars. Only $4,990 to go." She set her shoulders to brace herself for a boring evening of interrogation and dragged herself out of the house to visit her new family.

# Don't miss out!

Visit the website below and you can sign up to receive emails whenever R. A. Gates publishes a new book. There's no charge and no obligation.

https://books2read.com/r/B-A-FHKFC-SQVCG

**BOOKS 2 READ**

Connecting independent readers to independent writers.

# Also by R. A. Gates

Pucker Up
The Tenth Life of Mr. Whiskers
A Small Medium at Large
Pesto & Potions